TRIBES of NATIVE AMERICA

Apache

edited by Marla Felkins Ryan
and Linda Schmittroth

BLACKBIRCH®
PRESS

THOMSON

GALE

San Diego • Detroit • New York • San Francisco • Cleveland
New Haven, Conn. • Waterville, Maine • London • Munich

THOMSON

GALE

LIBRARY OF CONGRESS CATALOGING-IN-PUBLICATION DATA

Apache / Marla Felkins Ryan, book editor; Linda Schmittroth, book editor.
    p. cm. — (Tribes of Native America)
Includes bibliographical references and index.
  Contents: Name — History: trading and raiding — Economy: before the twentieth century — Chiricahua Apache — Cochise — Geronimo — Daily life — Customs: festivals and cemonies.
  ISBN 1-56711-604-3 (alk. paper)
  1. Apache Indians—Juvenile literature. [1. Apache Indians. 2. Indians of North America — New Mexico.] I. Ryan, Marla Felkins. II. Schmittroth, Linda. III. Series.
  E99.A6A59 2003
  979.004'972—dc21   2002008666

Printed in United States
10 9 8 7 6 5 4 3 2 1

Table of Contents

FIRST LOOK 4
Name
Location
Population
Origins and group ties

HISTORY 8
Trade and raids
Under U.S. control
Cochise and the Apache Wars
Geronimo
Chato
Victorio
Religion
Government: In the old times
On the reservation
  Apache Population: 1990
Economy: Traditional ways
  The Recreation Business
Modern economy

DAILY LIFE 19
Families
Buildings
Education
Food
Clothing
Healing practices
Crafts revival
Oral literature
  The Emergence: How The Apache Came To Earth

CUSTOMS 26
Festivals and ceremonies
Puberty
Courtship and marriage
Married life
War rituals
Death and burial
Current tribal issues
Notable people

For More Information 31

Glossary 32

Index 32

APACHE

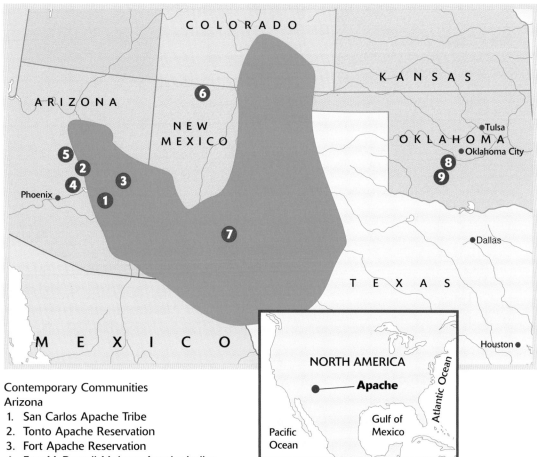

Contemporary Communities
Arizona
1. San Carlos Apache Tribe
2. Tonto Apache Reservation
3. Fort Apache Reservation
4. Fort McDowell Mohave-Apache Indian Community
5. Yavapai-Apache Tribe New Mexico
6. Jicarilla Apache Tribe
7. Mescalero Apache Tribe Oklahoma
8. Apache Tribe of Oklahoma
9. Fort Sill Apache Tribe of Oklahoma

Shaded area: Traditional lands of the Apache in present-day Arizona, New Mexico, Texas, northern Mexico, and southeastern Colorado.

Chiricahua Apache
Contemporary Communities
1. Mescalero Apache Reservation, New Mexico
2. Fort Sill Apache Reservation, Oklahoma

Shaded area: Traditional lands of the Chiricahua in present-day Arizona, New Mexico, and northern Mexico.

Name

Apache (pronounced *uh-PATCH-ee*). The name may come from the Zuñi word *apachu,* which means "enemy."

The name Chiricahua (pronounced CHEER-uh-KAH-wuh) may mean "chatterer." It may refer to the warriors' coded speech in battle. The Chiricahua call themselves *de Apache,* which means "man" or "person."

Location

Apache lands stretched from what is now central Arizona to central Texas, and from northern Mexico to southeastern Colorado. Today, about 30,000 Apache live on nine reservations in Arizona, New Mexico, and Oklahoma.

The Chiricahua Apache lived in mountainous areas of southeastern Arizona, southwestern New Mexico, and northern Mexico. Today, about 100 Chiricahua live in southwestern Oklahoma.

The Apache originally lived in what is now the southwestern United States.

Population

At the end of the 1600s, there were about 5,000 Apache. In a 1990 population count by the U.S. Bureau of the Census, 53,330 people said they were Apache.

In the early to mid-1800s, there were 2,500 to 3,000 Chiricahua. In 1886, there were just over 500. By 1990, only 17 Chiricahua lived in New Mexico. In the 1990 census, 739 people said they were Chiricahua.

An Apache silversmith

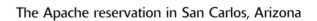

The Apache reservation in San Carlos, Arizona

Origins and group ties

The Apache moved from western Canada to the American Southwest between the 13th and 16th centuries. Today, they are divided into Western Apache and Eastern Apache. The Chiricahua are part of the Eastern Apache. The Apache are a proud, religious people. They may have resisted white settlement on their lands longer and more fiercely than any other tribe. Legendary figures Cochise, Chato, Geronimo, and Victorio and his sister Lozen were all Chiricahua Apache.

Tsoe, a White Mountain Apache, around 1885

•Timeline•

1540
Spanish gold seekers meet the Apache for the first time.

1607
Jamestown colony is settled.

1620
Mayflower lands at Plymouth, Massachusetts

1776
America declares independence from England.

1847
The Apache fall under American control.

1861
Cochise is arrested, and the Apache Wars begin.

1861
American Civil War begins

1865
Civil War ends.

1874
Cochise dies

HISTORY

Trade and raids

When the Spanish came to the Southwest in 1540, the Apache traded with them. Relations turned sour when the Spanish tried to take control of Apache land. The Apache began to attack Spanish settlements. Spanish explorers also passed by Chiricahua lands, but probably did not see the tribe's mountain homes.

By the late 1500s, the Spanish built settlements and missions in the Southwest. The Spanish soldiers made many Indians slaves. Missionaries tried to change their religion. Though all Apache disliked the Spanish, the Spanish found their worst enemies in the Chiricahua.

In 1786, the Spanish sent Comanche and Navajo warriors to hunt down Apache. The Spanish then bribed the Apache to settle near missions, stop their raids, and live in peace. One by one, Apache groups accepted the bribe. Some fled to the mountains, however, and kept up their raids.

Under U.S. control

In 1848, after the Mexican-American War, the United States won land that included Apache

Apache and Comanche fighters battled white buffalo hunters.

territory. The government soon made it clear that it would not put up with raids.

Between the 1850s and 1875, Apache groups were placed on reservations in Arizona and New Mexico. Then the government decided the reservations were too expensive. It tried to move all the Apache to the Mescalero Reservation in New Mexico and the San Carlos Reservation in Arizona. Fights broke out, and many Apache fled.

Cochise and the Apache Wars

Cochise (pronounced *coh-CHEES*; c. 1812-1874) is one of the best-known Chiricahua leaders. He moved to a reservation in 1853. In 1861, an army

1886
The surrender of Geronimo's band marks the end of Apache armed resistance to white settlement.

1913
The majority of surviving Chiricahua move to Mescalero Reservation in New Mexico.

1917–1918
WWI

1934
The Indian Reorganization Act gives tribes self-government.

1941
Bombing at Pearl Harbor forces U.S. into WWII.

1945
WWII ends.

1950s
Reservations no longer controlled by federal government.

Cochise was a well-known Apache leader.

Geronimo and his wife

officer arrested Cochise on a false kidnapping charge. He was taken prisoner with some companions. He escaped, but his people were murdered. This set off the Apache Wars.

Cochise and his followers fought white settlement until a white friend convinced him to move to a reservation and end the wars. Cochise died in 1874. After that, the Chiricahua were moved to the San Carlos Reservation in Arizona. They were very unhappy there, and some escaped. Another decade of battles began.

Geronimo

Geronimo (pronounced *juh-RON-uh-moe;* c. 1827-1909) was a medicine man and warrior. He believed that to be removed from one's homeland was to die.

When Mexican raiders killed his mother, wife, and children in 1858, Geronimo vowed vengeance. He was caught more than once and returned to the reservation. He would then escape again. He fought until General George H. Crook's troops captured him in 1886.

Geronimo (front row, second from right) and his men were captured in 1886.

Apache leader Alfred Chato rode with Geronimo.

Geronimo and his band were forced to move to Florida. Other Apache went to reservations in the Southwest.

Chato

Alfred Chato (c. 1860-1934) rode with Geronimo and also led his own raids. He was convinced to return to San Carlos with Geronimo in 1884.

There, Chato learned to farm. He also worked as a scout and consultant for the U.S. army. In 1886, government officials asked Chato for help. They wanted to convince the Chiricahua to move to Florida instead of their former lands, as originally planned. Chato refused. On his trip home, he was arrested and sent to Florida.

Conditions in Florida were very bad. In 1894, Chato and the other Chiricahua moved with Geronimo to Fort Sill, Oklahoma.

In 1913, Chato went to Washington again. He asked that his people be allowed to return to their homeland. After many discussions, the Apache eventually were offered a chance to go back to New Mexico.

In 1913, the Apache at Fort Sill were given a choice to make. They could stay in Oklahoma and receive 80 acres of land each, or return to New Mexico to live on the Mescalero Reservation. Eighty-seven stayed in Oklahoma. The other 171 went to New Mexico.

Victorio

Victorio (c. 1820-1880) was told in 1879 that his reservation at Warm Springs, New Mexico, would be opened for white settlement. He replied, "If you force me and my people to leave [Warm Springs], there will be trouble. Leave us alone, so that we may remain at peace."

He was trapped by Mexican soldiers, who killed 61 warriors and 18 women and children. Sixty others became slaves. Victorio killed himself rather than be taken prisoner.

Religion

The Apache are very religious. They seek the help of the gods before they hunt, farm, or go to war. The Apache believe in a creator called Ussen, or Life Giver. Friendly Mountain Spirits are worshipped in ceremonies led by leaders called shamans (pronounced *SHAH-munz* or *SHAY-munz*). Shamans also heal the sick. Spanish missionaries convinced many Apache to become Catholics. Still, they never left their old religion behind.

Many Apache religious ceremonies include dancing.

In 1881, an Apache medicine man named Nochedelklinne said he had a vision. In it, white men vanished and dead Apache came back to life. His vision included a dance that he taught to the Apache. White officials feared the dance might start an Indian revolution. Nochedelklinne was murdered by white soldiers in late 1881.

Christian missionaries from the Reformed Church in America came to Fort Sill in 1899. They set up schools, tended the sick, and held religious services. The church is still strong at Fort Sill.

Government

In the old times

The family is the most important Apache unit. Until the 20th century, the tribe had no central government. Instead, family groups usually acted on their own.

Sometimes family groups came together to make important decisions. The male heads of each family group formed a council. They talked over the problem, and then made a decision. Even if they decided to act together, however, the groups were never very large.

The family is the most important Apache unit.

Like other Apache, each small group of Chiricahua had a leader. He was admired for his wisdom, bravery, or his way of speaking. He had to consult the heads of other families to make decisions.

On the reservations

The government set up a U.S. Indian Police force to oversee law enforcement, health, and land use on reservations. Government agents mainly wanted to make the Indians act more like whites.

APACHE POPULATION: 1990

According to the U.S. Bureau of the Census, in 1990, 53,330 people said they were Apache. This made the tribe the country's seventh largest. The people identified themselves this way:

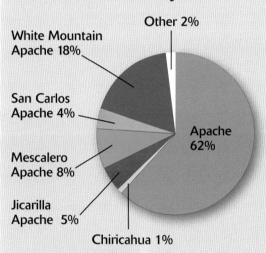

Other 2%

White Mountain Apache 18%

San Carlos Apache 4%

Mescalero Apache 8%

Jicarilla Apache 5%

Chiricahua 1%

Apache 62%

SOURCE: "1990 census of population and housing. Subject summary tape file (SSTF) 13 (computer file): characteristics of American Indians by tribe and language." Washington, DC: U.S. Department of Commerce, Bureau of the Census, Data User Services Division, 1995).

The Chiricahua and Fort Sill Apache are scattered throughout the United States. Below are the states with the largest Chiricahua populations.

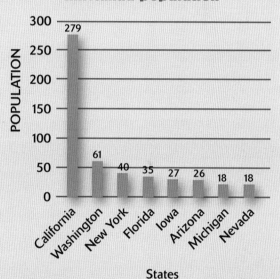

Chiricahua population

State	Population
California	279
Washington	61
New York	40
Florida	35
Iowa	27
Arizona	26
Michigan	18
Nevada	18

States

SOURCE: "Selected from American Indian Population by Selected Tribes: 1990, U.S. Bureau of the Census, 1990 Census of Population, Characteristics of American Indians by Tribe and Language," 1990, CP-3-7, Table 1.

In 1934, Congress passed the Indian Reorganization Act. Tribes were allowed to form elected tribal councils. This is the type of government the Apache still use today.

For a long time, the Fort Sill Apache had only an informal business council. When the U.S. government threatened to dissolve the tribe in the 1950s, it formed a tribal committee. In the 1970s, the Fort Sill Apache formed a new government with elected members.

The Apache stretched animal hides on racks like this one.

Economy

Traditional ways

In the early days, Apache made items from buffalo. Most often they made robes and jerky (meat cut into long strips and dried or cured with smoke). The Apache traded these for corn, beans, gourds, cotton cloth, and minerals.

Later, the Apache traded with the Spanish. They exchanged buffalo hides for grain, cattle, horses, and guns. They still made raids, however, to get what they wanted.

THE RECREATION BUSINESS

Several Apache tribes have taken advantage of interest in outdoor sports. Many Mescalero Apache work at their ski resort. Others work at the tribal museum and visitor center. The tourist center at Montezuma Castle National Monument—where the Yavapai Apache own 75 acres—is an important source of revenue. The Jicarilla Apache run a ski enterprise. Tourism creates jobs and brings money to many reservations.

White Mountain Apache Cultural Center, Fort Apache, Arizona

When the Apache moved to reservations in the late 1800s, they were expected to farm. The land was poor, though, and there was little water. Some Apache went to work for wages.

Modern economy

After World War I ended in 1918, the government encouraged the Apache to raise cattle. Some tribes have done so with great success. Others process lumber.

The Chiricahua Apache have a successful timber industry.

The Apache are known as fine rodeo performers.

Today, Apache work at many jobs. Some still farm and ranch. The Apache are also known as fine rodeo performers. On the Mescalero Reservation in New Mexico, the Chiricahua Apache have successful timber and tourist operations, including a luxurious resort.

The Fort Sill people have not done as well. When they moved to their own plots of land in 1913, they raised cattle and farmed. By the 1940s and 1950s, many Chiricahua could not afford to compete with other farms. They had to find work wherever they could. In the 1970s, the economy improved somewhat. Unemployment and poverty are still problems today, however.

DAILY LIFE

Families

Life revolved around the extended family. It included mother, father, children, grandparents, cousins, uncles, and aunts. All these people lived in single-family homes close together. Apache women had few children.

Buildings

The Apache usually built single-family homes called wickiups (pronounced *WIK-ee-ups*). These were cone- or dome-shaped structures. They had a framework of poles covered with brush, grass, reed mats, or skins.

Apache wickiups consisted of a pole framework covered with grass or other material.

The Chiricahua were mountain dwellers who moved often. In the summer, they lived in the cooler highlands. In the winter, they moved to the lowlands. Winter camps often had a sweat lodge for the men.

Education

To learn life skills, Apache children listened to, watched, and imitated their

Pine nuts were an important Apache food.

Some Apache children attended boarding schools where they were expected to be like whites.

parents. Both boys and girls learned how to run swiftly, how to ride horses, and how to sneak up on enemy villages.

On reservations, Apache children were expected to be like whites. Government and mission schools taught only in English.

Today, the Apache take an active interest in education. Some Apache schools have been singled out as model schools for their bilingual and bicultural programs.

Food

The Apache were hunter-gatherers. They hunted bison, antelope, deer, elk, cougars, mountain sheep, quail, and wild turkey. After the late 1600s, some Apache hunted buffalo.

They also gathered cactus fruits, pecans, acorns, black walnuts, pine nuts, chokecherries, juniper berries, and raspberries.

Chiricahua were also mainly hunter-gatherers. The men used bows and arrows to hunt deer, antelope, elk, mountain goats, and mountain sheep. To help out, small boys hunted rabbits, squirrels, birds, and opossums. Animals such as the badger and wildcat were hunted only for their skins.

Clothing

Apache men wore buckskin breechcloths, or garments with front and back flaps that hung from the waist. They also wore ponchos (blanket-like cloaks) and moccasins with attached leggings. Women wore buckskin skirts, ponchos, and moccasins. Men usually cut their hair shoulder-length and wore cloth headbands. Women wore their hair long.

The Chiricahua also wore clothing made of tanned animal skins. Because they lived near the Mexican border, they adopted some Mexican-style clothing. Men wore white cotton shirts, long white cotton breechcloths, and boot-like moccasins. In the later nineteenth century, they began to wear American-style black vests or jackets.

Apache men wore breechcloths and leggings, while women wore ponchos and skirts.

Women also adopted American clothing in the late nineteenth century. They wore long-sleeved blouses and full skirts with decorative borders at the bottom.

Healing practices

The Apache believed that evil spirits made people get sick. Shamans, who could be either male or female, used herbs, dances, and chants to cure people. The person who asked for aid sprinkled the shaman's head with pollen and offered a gift. The shaman took the gift only if he or she took the case. The shaman then sprinkled the patient with pollen and did a ritual with four dancers. The ceremony was repeated for four nights.

Sometimes sweat baths were used to cure colds and fever. The Apache set broken bones with splints made from cedar bark. Bleeding—the draining of blood from a sick person—was used for headaches.

The Chiricahua used healing herbs and roots. Mud baths were also used to treat many ailments. A hot cloth spread with grease and ash was sometimes used for diseases such as mumps.

By the end of the twentieth century, Apache health problems were often linked to poor diet and poverty. There were also very high rates of contagious diseases such as tuberculosis.

Crafts revival

The Apache take pride in traditional crafts. Basketry and pottery making had nearly died out by the 1950s. Now, however, they are valued skills that are taught and learned with great enthusiasm.

Apache baskets

Oral literature

The Apache keep their sacred stories about the creation of the universe and the supernatural secret. Some stories that have been written down include tales about the adventures of Coyote and Big Owl. Coyote is sometimes shown as a hero who taught the Apache how to take care of themselves. At other times, Coyote is a fool who suffers when he makes bad moral decisions.

Apache storytellers related tales of Coyote and Big Owl.

THE EMERGENCE:
HOW THE APACHE CAME TO EARTH

Long ago they say. Long ago they made the earth and the sky. There were no people living on the earth then. There were four places under the earth where Red Ants were living. These Red Ants were talking about this country up here on the surface of the earth, and they wanted to come up here. Among them was the Red Ant chief and he talked about coming here. "All right, let's go to this new place above!" all the Ants decided. There was a big cane growing in that place. This grew upwards toward the sky.

The Apache believed that porcupines (above) and badgers (opposite page) were among the first creatures on earth.

Then all the Red Ant People started off from the bottom of this cane and traveled up it. When they reached the first joint of the cane they made camp there all night. The next day they traveled on from there, still upwards.

They spent many nights on their way, always making their camp at the joints of the cane. They kept on traveling that way, upwards, and then finally the chief told them to look around this place where they were. So all the people went out and looked around this new country and all of them said that this was a nice place. There were lots of foods growing all around. The chief said, "Bring in all those foods that are good to eat, to our camp." So the people brought in the different kinds of foods and fruits that were good. They went all over the country for these wild foods. This way they found lots to eat and they found good places to live all over the new land.

After that the chief told the people to look around, and then he sang a song. At every song that he sang all the people were to come together again. Then the chief was singing and in his song he said, "You can go off any place you want to, and when you find a place that is good, then stop there and settle." So this was the first place that people were living, and these were the first people, the Red Ants.

Badger and Porcupine were the first ones on this earth also. Then all kinds of birds started to live on this earth; Eagle and Hawk and all the other kinds. Then God had made man on this earth and everyone was living well. This is the story about how man first became.

My yucca fruits lie piled up.

SOURCE: Bane Tithla, storyteller. "Hatc'onondai (the emergence, or the emerging place)." Myths and Tales of the White Mountain Apache. Glenville Goodwin. New York: American Folk-lore Society, 1939.

CUSTOMS

Festivals and ceremonies

Apache ceremonies celebrated important life events. These might include the naming of an infant, a child's first pair of moccasins, a first haircut, or puberty. There could be hundreds of ceremonies each year.

One Apache ceremony celebrated a child's first pair of moccasins.

Most rituals used pollen and the number four. Pollen is a symbol of life, fertility, and beauty. The number four represents the four directions—north, south, east, and west.

To keep in touch with other native nations, the Fort Sill Apache host rodeos and powwows that feature traditional songs and dances. The singers and dancers at powwows today come from many tribes.

Puberty

A girl's coming-of-age was a major ceremony. Part of it was called the Dance of the Mountain Spirits. In it, masked people pretended to be gods of the mountains. The honored girl played the role of White Painted

Apache dancers perform the Dance of the Mountain Spirits.

Woman, who is like Mother Earth. The dance was supposed to bring good luck to the whole tribe.

A boy's puberty ceremony came through his first four raids on enemy settlements. After he completed them, he was seen as an adult.

Courtship and marriage

There was little contact between young Apache women and men. Dances gave them rare chances to meet.

A young man's whole family chose his bride. His parents or their representatives offered gifts to the girl's parents. If they accepted the gifts, the couple was often considered married with little or no further ceremony.

The Apache performed many dances. This photo shows the Crown Dance.

Married life

Married couples lived near the wife's parents. The Apache believed marriage would be happier if the wife's mother had no contact at all with her son-in-law.

A man had to take care of his wife's family. If she died, he had to marry her sister or a single cousin. Some prosperous men might have several wives.

War rituals

The Apache asked for help from the gods before a battle. In a special ceremony, dancers acted out the brave deeds they hoped to perform. If the battle was won, they acted out their achievements in another dance.

War parties sometimes had as many as 100 warriors.

War parties might have up to 100 warriors. These small groups bravely faced much larger forces. When a cause seemed hopeless, warriors scattered. They did not fight to the death.

Death and burial

After death, a corpse's face was painted red. The body was wrapped in skins and removed as soon as possible. It was loaded on a horse, taken to a cave or other remote area, and put in a tomb. Survivors did not go near the burial ground. They never again spoke the name of the dead person.

Current tribal issues

Poverty is a constant concern, but some Apache solutions have raised controversy. For example, in 1996, the Mescalero Apache took a contract to hold nuclear waste at their reservation. They said the contract would bring jobs. Critics said it could lead to disaster.

Another issue is the seizure of Apache lands. The Jicarilla Apache won nearly $10 million in a lawsuit for land unjustly taken from them. The United States would not return the land, however.

At Fort Sill, Chiricahua trace Apache genealogy (ancestry). They also try to revive parts of their culture that began to vanish as tribal members moved away in the 1940s and 1950s.

Tonto Apache tribal office near Payson, Arizona

Notable People

Allan Houser (1914-1994) was a Chiricahua Apache sculptor. He was famous for his work in wood, marble, stone, and bronze.

Lozen (c. 1840s-1886) was the sister of war leader Victorio. She was a medicine woman and horsewoman who rode into battle with Victorio and later Geronimo.

Other notable Apache include scholar Veronica E. Velarde Tiller; Apache-Hopi-Pueblo author Michael Lacapa; poet and educator Jose Garza; and poet and short-story-writer Lorenzo Baca.

For More Information

Buchanan, Kimberly Moore. "Apache Women Warriors." *Southwestern Studies* No. 79. Debo, Angie.

Geronimo. *Geronimo: His Own Story.* Edited by Frederick W. Turner III. New York: Dutton, 1970.

McKissack, Patricia. *The Apache. A New True Book. Chicago:* Children's Press, 1984.

Melody, Michael E. *The Apache.* New York: Chelsea House, 1989.

Roberts, David. *Once They Moved Like the Wind: Cochise, Geronimo, and the Apache Wars.* New York: Simon & Schuster, 1993.

Sweeney, Edwin R. *Cochise: Chiricahua Apache Chief.* Norman: University of Oklahoma Press, 1991.

White, Julia. *Lozen-Chiricahua Apache.* http://www.twelvestring.com/innerspace/lozen.htm

Glossary

Mission a local church or parish dependent on a larger religious organization for direction or financial support

Reservation land set aside and given to Native Americans

Ritual something that is custom or done in a certain way

Shaman a priest or priestess who uses magic for the purpose of curing the sick, divining the hidden, and controlling events

Treaty agreement

Tribe a group of people who live together in a community

Index

Apachu, 5

Bleeding, 22
Breechcloths, 21

Chato, Alred, 11-12
Cochise, 7, 9-10
Crook, George H., 10

Death, 29

Family groups, 14
Fort Sill, 12, 13, 15, 16, 18, 26, 30

Indian Reorganization Act, 16

Jerky, 16

Medicine man, 10
Mescalero Reservation, 9, 12, 18
Mexican-American War, 8-9
Missionaries, 8, 13
Moccasins, 21, 26

Montezuma Castle National Monument, 17

Nochedelklinne, 13

Pollen, 26
Ponchos, 21
Pow wows, 26

Red ants, 24-25
Reformed Church, 13
Rodeo, 18

San Carlos Reservation, 9, 10
Shamans, 13, 22

U.S. Bureau of the Census, 6, 15
U.S. Indian Police Force, 14
Ussen, 13

Warm Springs, NM, 12
White Painted Woman, 26-27
Wickiups, 19

J970.3 APACHE
Apache

7

**DAY
BOOK**

$26.19

DATE			
CHILDREN'S DEPARTMENT			
INDIAN BOOKS			
7 DAYS ONLY			
NO RENEWALS			

BAKER & TAYLOR